SACRIFICES

Edgar Waldgrave

SACRIFICES

The Witch Chronicles

Rise of the Dark Witch High King

Book One

Hometown Publishers

Hometown Publishers
www.hometownpublishers.com

First Published by Hometown Publishers July, 2020.

ISBN: 978-1-7770337-2-9 (Paperback)
ISBN: 978-1-7770337-3-6 (E-book)

Library and Archives Canada (LAC) national library collection.

Cover Design by Edgar Waldgrave.

Dedication

To B, D,

J, & M

To my dad and mom,

C & M

Acknowledgements

Thank you for reading my fictional account

of The Witch Chronicles as they pertain to

the White, Gray, Black, and Dark Witches

of the Northeast Region of the United States.

Please note that the towns of Amare,

Seneca County, and Charlotte, Cayuga County,

even though described and geographically

portrayed as being in the State of New York,

are fictitious.

Thank you to all the people and establishments,

in the eleven Northeast States in the USA.

Enjoy...

Eleanor Peabody
August 6, 1975

The Witch Trial

"Breaking news," interrupted the anchorman," we have a verdict in the Eleanor Peabody trial, let's go to Brooke live at the Boston Municipal Courthouse, Brooke?"

"Thank you, Harvey, yes, a verdict was read by the head juror minutes ago. And after only several hours of deliberations, they have come back with a 'not guilty' verdict against all three men charged in the first-degree murder of Eleanor Peabody, that took place almost a year ago, on August 6, 1975. Harvey?"

"Brooke, 'The Witch Trial,' as it has been dubbed, has been a media sensation from day one. But perhaps for the benefit of our viewers who haven't been privy to the courtroom drama, you could highlight the events leading up to this dramatic outcome today."

"Of course, Harvey," replied Brooke pushing her hair away from her face. "The night before her death, Eleanor Peabody and the three accused men, were seen partying in several bars throughout downtown Boston. During testimony, staff and customers corroborated the defense's case that Mrs. Peabody was, although drunk, lucid enough to carry on conversations with not only the three men but also staff and several customers that knew her. They also confirmed the accused men's accounts that throughout the night Eleanor Peabody claimed to be a witch, who not only actively practiced witchcraft, but also black magic. She was also seen kissing each of the three men on different occasions. And at the last bar, several staff and customers recalled her inviting the accused men

1

over to her place for an after-party, where she promised them booze, drugs, and sex."

"So, Brooke, how did the prosecution counter these detrimental allegations?"

"Harvey, the prosecution has always asserted that Eleanor Peabody was either sedated or drugged prior to entering the first bar, and had several witnesses counter previous accusations, by saying that Eleanor Peabody did not know where she was, was inarticulate and stumbling. But surveillance video of the victim walking in and out of the bars on her own, proved otherwise."

"And what happened after the four of them left that last bar?" asked Harvey, leading her on.

"Eleanor Peabody and the three men went back to her apartment and partied till the early hours of August 6. Neighbors testified that they heard the four of them listening to music, talking, laughing, and engaging in sex. This also strengthened the defense's case, proving that the sex was consensual, and substantiated the coroner's report that she wasn't raped. The prosecution in turn, said with Eleanor Peabody being drugged, she would be unresponsive to the men's advances, and therefore, there would be no signs of forcible entry. To which the coroner concurred was also a possibility. The prosecution asked him further about the amount of alcohol and drug levels found in the victim's toxicology report, and based on those findings, was she even capable of saying no to the men or even fighting them off. The coroner concluded, with the elevated levels found in her system, it may be a possibility, but also added that each person has their own tolerance level to alcohol and drugs, and if she had done this on a regular basis, she may have been impervious to these excessive amounts, and in fact, quite coherent."

"Brooke, to the allegations of whether she was coherent or not, a key witness seemed to be, just that, key. How did his testimony play out?"

"Yes, Harvey, just when it seemed the prosecution was gaining some momentum, the most damaging witness of all was the young man returning home from work, who not only saw the three men leaving Eleanor's apartment, but her saying goodbye to them before closing her door. When the prosecution questioned the witness, they really seemed to be concentrating on what he had actually heard and seen, as opposed to what he thought he had. In their argument, the prosecution was claiming that the witness never saw the victim, and only heard a female voice and her door closing, and therefore, only observed the three accused men walking by him. The defense countered that by saying, in either case, the men were heard and seen leaving while the victim was still alive. The prosecution argued that without facial recognition, the voice may have not been Eleanor Peabody's, but a fourth individual inside the apartment impersonating her, and that she had been murdered prior to the three men seen leaving."

"What about a witness coming forward and saying he had seen someone leaving from the back-window apartment on the third floor, apparently Eleanor Peabody's apartment, and then walking down the alley?"

"Yes, this did support the prosecution's argument that a fourth individual was involved in her murder and perhaps left via the back stairwell. Unfortunately, the witness, Gordy Jacobs, a homeless alcoholic, was stabbed and killed three months ago from an apparent burglary gone wrong. Even though his testimony was allowed, not having him appearing at the trial, was a blow to the prosecution."

"Brooke, can you quickly describe to our viewers how the victim was found early that morning?"

"Harvey, at around seven, Eleanor Peabody was discovered in her bedroom lying on a white sheet with a black pentacle sprayed on it. Her body had been cut with a knife, from her pubic mound up to her chin, and then from ear to ear, with her hand still clutching the knife that was used."

"What were the defense and prosecution's positions as to the cause of this ritualistic-type death?"

"The defense stated that it only strengthened their claims that she was a witch, who practiced witchcraft and black magic, and ultimately sacrificed her body, and in the words of the defense, 'to Satan.' The prosecution had several witnesses testify that they were very close to Eleanor Peabody and maintained she never practiced witchcraft or black magic. The prosecution went on to say, because of these witnesses' testimony and the lack of substantial evidence, Eleanor Peabody was not a witch, and she did not practice witchcraft or black magic. And that the sheet with the black pentacle painted on it, had to have been planted by the accused, to fabricate the truth behind their well-planned execution. A notion that the defense swiftly rebutted by restating their previous witnesses' testimonies: that the victim had openly admitted to being a witch who practiced witchcraft and black magic. Harvey?"

"So, with the witness testimonies ending, this set the stage for closing arguments, right Brooke?" asked Harvey, moving it along.

"Yes, in their closing arguments, the prosecution still maintained that the three men, along with a fourth who was let in through the back window, were responsible for Eleanor Peabody's 'thrill-kill' murder. Which came across as weak, unsubstantiated, and inconclusive. The defense stood behind what they considered the facts: that the three men were invited to Eleanor Peabody's apartment, partied with her, had consensual sex, and left early the following morning while she was alive. The defense also reminded the jury that the prosecution had failed to conclusively provide any substantial evidence, not only that the three accused men had killed Eleanor Peabody, but a motive as to why. And were desperately clutching at straws with their 'thrill-kill' murder theory. The defense continued by saying, that the reason the prosecution was struggling to find a motive, was because the three men were innocent. The defense finished their argument by saying, based on all the testimony the jury had heard, the only conclusion that they could make, was that the three accused men are innocent, and without a shadow of a doubt, deserve a verdict of, 'not guilty.'…And that sadly, on the morning of August 6, 1975, Eleanor Peabody took her own life…After making this point, the defense attorney paused momentarily and ended his argument by saying, it's now time for the jury to end this trial and let those who knew Eleanor Peabody be allowed to mourn her passing. Which was very touching and emotional, Harvey?"

"Yes, it was, and I'm sure those who were close to her, would like nothing more than to put all this behind them and mourn her loss," replied Harvey sympathetically. "Brooke, one final question, how was the verdict met in the courtroom after it was read?"

"With this trial there has been several scandals surrounding it, the most notable ones being questions arising of witnesses being paid off, tampering of evidence, and the sudden death of the homeless man, Gordy Jacobs. Even with none of them ever proven, it did leave a tarnish on this trial and its proceedings. With that being said, there was a mix of emotions this afternoon after the verdict was read. The family and friends of the accused cheered; while those of the victim were very subdued, in shock, and noticeably upset, with several of them crying. Eleanor Peabody's twenty-five-year-old daughter, the person who found her deceased mother that fateful morning, abruptly left the courtroom surrounded by family and friends, and was visibly shaken and sobbing."

"Quite understandable," suggested Harvey empathetically.

"Yes, it is, and it must have been, and still is, a tragic event for this young woman to have not only witnessed, but endured this past year, and without a doubt for the rest of her life…our hearts go out to her."

"They most certainly do," said Harvey solemnly.

"One second, Harvey, I have the lead defense attorney, Mr. Ernest Cartwright heading my way," said Brooke waving to get his attention. "Mr. Cartwright, Mr. Cartwright, what do you have to say about the verdict today?"

"Brooke, I have always maintained that these men were innocent, and it was my responsibility to show, not convince, the jury of that, also."

"After only several hours of deliberations, what are your thoughts on the jurors coming back so quickly with their verdict?"

"The jury's swift response of a 'not guilty' verdict on all counts, states to me, and the public, that they believed these men were, without a doubt, innocent. I would also like to add, Brooke, that this is not only a triumphant day for these three men, but for the city of Boston, the state of Massachusetts, and our country's legal system; the best in the world…Thank you."

"Thank you, Mr. Cartwright," replied Brooke. "There you have it, back to you in the studio, Harvey."

"Well, to quickly recap, the three men charged with the first-degree murder of Eleanor Peabody, have been found 'not guilty,' on all counts," reiterated Harvey. "Now, in business news—"

A man in the Fairmont Copley Plaza suite turned off the television, walked over to the window, and looked down at Copley Square, thinking. His thoughts were suddenly interrupted by the ringing of the phone, and casually strolled over and picked it up. "Hello," he said, then listened. "You did a magnificent job, Ernest, and your interview with Brooke was the icing on the cake. And it is, without a doubt, a triumphant day…Of course, go and enjoy your celebration dinner with your legal team tonight, and I'll meet you tomorrow evening downstairs in the lobby bar…Seven is fine, we'll have a few celebratory drinks, and then go for steak, lobster, and champagne. On me, of course…Ernie, you deserved every penny, in fact, I'm so happy with the outcome I have an additional six-figure cash bonus just for you. Let's just say it's my way of thanking you for a job well done…You're welcome, and I'll see you tomorrow at seven." He placed the phone down, walked back to the window, and looked out at the skyline. Catching his thirty-one-year-old reflection he smiled at himself narcissistically, for he knew he had flawlessly orchestrated it to perfection, and that Eleanor Peabody was not only the first, she was the beginning.

The Thief

Outside, the figure in the shadows peeked through the slightly opened window, then watched as Maggie undressed and put on her robe, before walking over to her phone, picking it up, and dialing a number. He listened in as the twenty-six-year-old told her fiancé that she was jumping in the shower and had left the front door unlocked for them. After hanging up she departed the room, and the figure in the darkness crept along the wall to her bathroom window, and peered inside as she turned on the shower, undressed, and stepped into the tub. The shadowy figure returned to her bedroom window, slowly opened it, and quietly climbed inside. He searched her bedroom placing jewelry into his sack, then rifled through her handbag taking money from her wallet, before proceeding into the living room and removing antique silverware and rare gold coins from the cabinet and adding them to his sack. Hearing the shower turn off, he suddenly stopped, crept silently back into the bedroom, and hid behind the door. Minutes later, Maggie came into the bedroom happily humming, she felt something prick the back of her neck, and before she knew what it was, collapsed unconsciously to the floor.

Fifteen minutes later, Maggie groggily woke up, and slowly began to piece together what had happened. She tried to move her arms but couldn't, and looked up at her right hand, it was firmly tied to the bedpost, as was her left to the other. She quickly glanced down at her feet bound to the posts at the end of her bed and frantically tried to kick herself free. Realizing she was securely fastened, she screamed, but the duct tape covering her mouth only muffled her desperate cries for help.

The thief in the living room, upon hearing her struggle, finished turning over the rest of the furniture, then went back into the bedroom. "Ah, finally awake," he said pleasantly.

Maggie watched the man, wearing a balaclava and dressed in black, walk over to her and sit on the edge of the bed. She begged him to let her go and leave her alone, but all that came out were garbled sounds.

"There, there, it will all be over soon," he said consolingly. "But first, let's have a talk." No sooner had the words come out of his mouth, he heard someone trying to open the front door, and looked over at the bedroom clock. "Oh, they're early," he said disappointedly. The thief walked out of the bedroom, gazed down the hallway, and saw a figure outside talking to another. They're probably wondering why the door is locked, he thought with a smile, then swiftly went back into the bedroom, pulled out a black-handled knife with a gold blade, and headed towards the bed. "My apologies, we won't have time for that chat."

Upon seeing the knife, Maggie desperately tried to free herself but couldn't. The thief watched her and patiently waited till she tired. Eventually she stopped, and looking into his black eyes, she pleaded with him for her life.

The man in black undid her robe, then inserted the knife into her pubic mound and sliced his way up to her chin. Maggie screamed in pain as the tears rolled down her face. The thief smiled, removed the knife, and meticulously slit her throat from ear to ear. He then stood up, placed the knife in his sack, and left through the open window, deliberately leaving blood stains on the sill. Outside, the thief threw a black case containing needles onto the lawn, and then quickly jumped over the back-garden fence before walking across the neighbor's garden to the side of the unoccupied house.

Standing on the corner of a black sheet, that he had laid out thirty minutes earlier, he removed his balaclava, hastily undressed, and threw the items in the middle of the sheet. He then took the knife out of his sack, placed it by his feet, and flung the sack containing the stolen goods on top of the pile of clothes. From a garbage bag the thief pulled out disinfectant, removed his surgical gloves and placed them on top of the sack, then cleaned his knife and hands thoroughly before tossing the disinfectant on top of the pile. He gently positioned the knife into a clear plastic bag and carefully put it into the side pocket of his gym bag, before removing another pair of surgical gloves and putting them on. Taking the four corners of the sheet, he lifted them up, trapping the clothes, gloves, stolen items, and disinfectant in the middle, before tying a strong knot and placing it into the garbage bag, and then tying that. The thief removed an outfit from his gym bag, got dressed, put on a Red Sox baseball cap, then removed his gloves and put them inside his jacket pocket. He cautiously opened the side gate and looked around methodically. Seeing that it was all clear, he picked up his gym bag and placed its strap over his shoulder then grabbed the garbage bag. After walking through the gate, he closed it behind him, and leisurely strolled to his car two streets over.

The thief nonchalantly placed the two bags into his trunk, then drove for ten minutes before stopping at a popular bar in Worcester. Here, he removed the garbage bag from the trunk, along with the gloves from his pocket, and threw them into the bar's dumpster before going inside for a few drinks and a conversation.

The following morning, a garbage truck pulled up to the bar's dumpster, emptied it, then continued on to the next building.

Jason Campbell
September 6, 1980

The Suicide

The Post-Standard, Syracuse, New York

September 7, 1980

Suspected child killer Jason Campbell

commits suicide,

by William Duncan

Town of Amare - The body of twenty-nine-year-old Jason Campbell was found last night at his place of residence in Seneca County. Deputies arrived at his home last night at 10 p.m. to arrest him for the murder of two young girls, when they found the gruesome discovery. Sources close to the investigation said that the suspect had carved himself with a knife from pubic mound to chin, and from ear to ear. The knife used was found at the scene, along with a suicide note left on top of several witchcraft and black magic books. Deputy Sheriff Lee Davidson summarized the note by saying it stated his sorrow for killing Amanda Peterson aged 11, and Heather Downs aged 12, who had gone missing two and six months earlier, respectively. A reliable source revealed that Jason Campbell also wrote in his wordy note, that he was a 'Servant of Satan,' and 'was called to sacrifice innocence in His name.' The local townspeople were shocked, not only to learn of his being charged with the murders, but his admission of guilt, and that he had actively practiced witchcraft and black magic, and had offered the young girls to Satan. It was also confirmed by Deputy Sheriff Lee

Davidson, that there was nothing in his note disclosing the location of the young girls' bodies. The investigation is still ongoing, and a news conference with further details is scheduled today at 2 p.m., at the Amare Townhall.

Beth Miller
Present Day – June 6

The Killing

Beth picked up her cell phone and dialed.

"Hello, beautiful," said a voice on the other end.

Beth blushed. "Hi, Jim, it's been slow here tonight, so I'll be ready at nine."

"Okay, I'll see you then, love you."

"Love you, too!" Beth hung up the phone, grabbed her handbag then happily sauntered to the back of the store, and went into the bathroom. She stood in front of the mirror and played with her hair for a moment before putting on some lipstick and admiring herself; she was a pretty, brown-haired girl with an attractive figure, and a cute smile. After giving herself an approving look, Beth glanced at her phone and read, '8:55.' She walked to the front of the store, set the alarm, turned off the lights, then closed and locked the door behind her as she went outside.

Beth looked up at the stars in the sky and took in a deep breath; the cool, spring air was refreshing. As dead leaves circled past her in harmony, she glanced down, and watched them dance into the darkness of the usually lit small parking lot. She wondered why the light was out, but thought nothing more of it, and strolled over to the bakery next door and read the sign, 'Closed early for family emergency, back in the morning.' Beth hoped Mrs. Johnson was okay. She continued past the bakery and peeked through the window of the dry cleaners. "Applegate's are still on their two-week cruise," she whispered, and thought about how romantic it would be to go on one. She resumed her walk, then realized something terrible and suddenly stopped, she was all alone.

She considered going back inside the boutique but quickly talked herself out of it. "Jim will be here any minute, he's never late," she said calming herself down, "besides, the alarm is set, and if it goes off, I would have to wait for security." Instead, Beth decided to amuse herself by walking back and forth in front of the stores and counting the number of steps.

"Sixty-nine, seventy," she said playfully, after reaching the end and turning around to go back. Behind her the flash of a shadow caught the corner of her eye. Before she could react, a cloth covered her mouth and nose, followed by a sickly-sweet smell, then sleep.

With ease the Northeast Butcher placed Beth over his shoulder, then quickly looked around, "no one," he whispered. He strolled to the back of the building, placed Beth in the trunk of his car, and glanced around once more, before jumping onto the front seat and removing his balaclava. Slowly he drove to the exit of the parking lot, "not a car in sight," he said with a smirk as he turned onto the main road. The Northeast Butcher patiently drove north for thirty minutes, pulled into a cemetery, and drove to the back next to a remote wooded area where he parked the car, put down the window, watched and listened. "No signs of life," he whispered as he put his balaclava back on and got out of his car.

He placed Beth over one shoulder, a sports bag over the other, and then walked for fifteen minutes into the deep thick woods before arriving at a small clearing. Here, he dropped the bag and laid Beth down gently, then slowly removed her clothes and placed them in his bag. He tied Beth's hands around one tree, and her feet to another, before placing duct tape over her mouth. Beth moaned as she started to come to. The Northeast Butcher stood over her and smiled as he thought about poor Jim wondering why his car wouldn't start, and old Mr. Johnson scurrying home to comfort his wife from the prowler she had seen in their yard.

Beth was now fully awake, after quickly realizing what was happening, she franticly tried to free herself. The Northeast Butcher squatted over her and shined the flashlight into her dark brown eyes, and in a calm voice whispered, "don't worry, in eight minutes you will be dead." Out of the bag he pulled out a knife with a black handle and a shiny, sharp, gold blade, and displayed it in front of her crying eyes. Beth's head jerked back and forth, as if to say, "no, please, no," but her fear only excited him. He grabbed her hair and spoke with enthusiastic delight. "I am going to slice your body, from here," he said placing the point of the knife on her pubic mound, "to here," he said moving it up to her stomach, then between her breasts, before stopping at her chin. "But that won't kill you." He let go of her hair, put down the knife, reached into his bag, and pulled out a small container. "Next, I will gently squirt this charcoal lighter fluid on you…but only where I've cut you," he explained motioning up and down the length of her nubile body. "And then I'll light it," he said taking in a deep breath, "I love the smell of burning flesh, and the crackling, bubbling sound it makes." Beth desperately struggled to get free, but the Northeast Butcher just sat and waited patiently till she fatigued. "But that won't kill you," he said putting the container down and picking up a handful of dirt, "after I put out the fire with this," he said throwing it to one side and pointing to her neck, "I will cut your throat from ear to ear. Then…then you will be dead."

There was a long silence as he sat and stared at her, before slowly standing and saying, "time to start praying." He angled the light onto her body, picked up the knife, and started carving. Several minutes later he reached over to sever Beth's jugular, she looked deep into his black eyes, and then felt the sharp knife slicing across her throat.

The Northeast Butcher packed up his bag then trekked back to his car. He removed the knife, cleaned it thoroughly, wrapped it in a cloth, and hid it under his spare tire. He took off his balaclava, the plastic covers from the seats and trunk, his oversize boots, his clothes, and bloodied surgical gloves, and placed them into his bag, then put on another pair, his suit, socks, and shoes. He placed his sports bag and the sheet he had been standing on, inside a garbage bag, tied it up, and threw it into the trunk, before removing his surgical gloves and putting them into his pocket. In twenty minutes, he would arrive at a trendy bar in Auburn, throw the garbage bag and gloves into its dumpster, then go inside for a drink and a chat. Tomorrow morning a garbage truck would arrive, empty it, and the bag and gloves would never be seen again.

As he drove out of the cemetery, the rain started slowly at first then began to pour, and if the weatherman was right, it would continue all night. The Northeast Butcher proudly smiled, turned on the music, and sang.

The Family

Henry Reed reached over and turned off the bedside alarm that he had set for six, it was only five-thirty, but his adrenalin was still pumping from last night. He quickly glanced over at Samantha who was sound asleep, before getting up, turning on the nightlight and walking over to the treadmill. Usually Henry would do sixty minutes; today he would do ninety. As he ran, he gazed at Sam and the cotton sheet clinging to her well-rounded breasts and firm buttocks. After three daughters, she still had the same figure from their wedding day, twenty years ago. He looked over at the dresser and smiled at the picture of him, Sam, and the three girls in front of the Magic Kingdom Castle. Henry thanked the Lord every day for his blessings, and today was no exception.

Ninety minutes later the treadmill stopped, Henry ran his fingers through his wet hair, stepped off, and crossed the room into the en suite. He was almost finished showering when the bathroom door opened.

"Only a half hour today?" asked Sam coming in and leaning against the wall.

Henry glided the glass shower door open. "No, I've been up since five-thirty, an hour and a half today," he replied with a smile. "I thought I'd spend some time with the girls this morning, have breakfast together, then we'd go to church and do something with them afterwards."

"They would like that," said Sam smiling approvingly. "How did your meeting go?"

"Excellent! I'm working on their proposals tomorrow," he said enthusiastically. "Landing this client would give our town national exposure and put us on the Finger Lake Region map as one of the most sought out places to live, and for tourists to visit."

"Well, if anybody can do it honey, it's you," she said proudly.

Henry leaned out and gave her a kiss. "I hope you didn't wait up too late for me last night?"

She had, but lied. "No, the girls and I watched a movie, and then we had an early night." Sam closed the shower door, turned to the basin, and brushed her teeth. Over the past six months, Henry had been working late hours, several nights a week, plus the occasional Saturdays. Then there were the bi-monthly weekend trips out of state. She knew better than anyone that Henry's hard work had landed many lucrative contracts for the company, and the recognition he received and deserved, was in the form of a promotion to VP of Land Development. And with his increase in salary, and cash bonuses, they were able to upgrade to a new house on the lake, buy a speedboat, and go on a spring-break vacation to Disney World. Even the town was benefiting considerably from the work he was doing, and Henry was absolutely right, Charlotte would not only be a beautiful place for people to live, but a hot tourist destination...Still, she missed him not being home, and didn't like sleeping alone, but deep down she knew she couldn't complain. Suddenly her thoughts were interrupted by the shower turning off. "I'll go wake up the girls and cook some breakfast," she said giving him a kiss and leaving.

"Smells good," said Vicky entering the kitchen and peeking over her mother's shoulder, "mmm, bacon and pancakes." She kissed her mother softly on the cheek then went to the fridge. "What time did Dad come home last night?"

"Glad I'm missed."

Vicky looked at her suited father standing in the doorway and turned to her mother teasingly. "Who's this young stud, Mom? Does Dad know about this guy?"

"What your father doesn't know won't hurt him," replied Sam playfully. "I think I'll keep this one, for now."

Henry walked over to Sam and in the voice of a mob boss, impishly said, "you are a beautiful, sexy, broad," then theatrically breathed in the aroma of the cooking food, "who is also a wonderful chef…your husband must be insane to leave you alone as much as he does. So, I will dispose of him and take his place, no?"

"He's crazy all right," said Sam as she rotated her index finger around the side of her head and made a comical face.

They all laughed.

"I'll have a glass of that orange juice, Victoria," said Henry as he sat down.

Vicky poured one for him and nervously looked over at her mother who motioned with her eyes to ask him. She placed the glass in front of her dad then sat down next to him. "Dad, can I ask you something?"

Henry noticed the nervousness in her voice and glanced at Sam, by her expression, she already knew. He looked back at his daughter and replied in the most reassuring tone possible. "Of course, honey, what is it?"

"Before you answer, let me finish, okay?"

Henry nodded with a smile.

"Remember eight months ago when we talked about me having a part time job, and you said when I was older, we would talk about it. Well," she hesitated, "there's one that's available at the library." She stopped and waited anxiously.

Henry looked deep into his daughter's green eyes; she reminded him so much of Sam. He really should have let her work last year when she asked, but he had his reasons. He looked over at Sam and could sense she had already given her approval, then turned to his daughter and placed his hand affectionately on her cheek. "Okay."

"Yes!" yelled Vicky joyfully as she jumped up and gave her dad a big hug and a kiss.

"But, on a couple of conditions."

"What conditions?" she asked, sitting down, her joy quickly evaporating.

"You leave your work schedule on the fridge, you keep your cell phone on at all times so we can reach you anytime, and you call for a ride home if it's late."

Her happiness quickly returned. "Agreed," she promised as she gave her dad a tight hug. Out of her bathrobe pocket she produced the training schedule for the next week, showed it to her dad, and then stuck it under the Mickey Mouse magnet on the fridge. "I start this afternoon, one till five." Vicky picked up a piece of toast, her orange juice, and proceeded out of the kitchen with an air of confidence and a smile on her face.

Henry watched her leave then looked back at Sam. "She's definitely your daughter!"

Sam walked to the table and put down his plate of food. "You're doing the right thing; besides, she is eighteen, and she needs some independence," said Sam reassuringly and kissing the top of his head.

"I know," he replied hesitantly, "it's not Victoria that worries me, it's the creeps out there."

"But we can't lock her up in this house forever," acknowledged Sam sympathetically.

"Not forever, just till she's…thirty-five," kidded Henry with a grin. He grabbed Sam, pulled her onto his lap, and quickly changed the subject. "When do we get to meet her new squeeze, Matt?"

Sam laughed at her husband trying to sound cool. "Tomorrow night, after we get back from the play. He's picking Vicky up from work and coming in to say hello." She then looked lovingly into her husband's blue eyes and kissed him passionately.

The Man

Driving to school, Henry thought about Victoria being eighteen and working, then turned to Megan and Stephanie asking them to reconfirm their ages.

"Daddy," replied Megan, "I'm thirteen, and Stephanie is fifteen."

Henry smiled to himself and thought, still a few more years before complete chaos.

"Don't forget my play starts at six tonight?" reminded Stephanie.

"I'll be on time," promised Henry. "Is it *Hamlet*...to be, or not to be?"

"Oh Daddy, we're doing *Beauty and the Beast*!"

He dropped the girls off with a kiss and waved as he watched them walk through the school doors. Driving away, he slowed down by the volunteer crossing guard. "Good morning, Joyce, another beautiful sunny day, and a great day to be alive."

She looked down at him. "Amen to that Mr. Reed. After I'm finished here, I'm taking a walk down to the park to feed the ducks in the pond, then sit on my favorite bench and watch those beautiful spring flowers bloom."

"I envy you Joyce," he said with a smile, "I wish I could join you."

"You're more than welcome anytime," she replied sincerely.

He said, "goodbye," and waved his hand out the window as he drove away.

She waved back, and thought, without Mr. Henry Reed there would be no park or pond for us pensioners to visit, bless his kind heart.

Henry spent the day in his office, working on the proposals for the new building site. At five, Rose, his executive assistant, knocked on the door to say goodnight and remind him of Stephanie's play. He thanked her, put on his coat, and walked her to her car. As Rose drove away, she looked at him through the rear-view mirror and thought to herself, how lucky she was to have him as her manager. He was kind, generous, and always thanked her for her hard work, and even promoted her from administrative assistant when he was promoted to vice president. He was a great boss, a gentle soul, and a loving family man.

The Play

Henry arrived as the play was just about to begin and sat next to Megan and Sam. During the intermission, the girls remained in the foyer while Henry went outside for some fresh air. He looked at his watch, seven o'clock, another hour to go, he thought. There was a tap on his back, Henry turned around and faced Deputy Sheriff Joe Murphy.

"Hello, Henry, how are you doing?"

"Good Joe, you?"

"I'm doing as well as can be expected, under the circumstances," he replied in a low voice, as they slowly walked away from the entrance. "I just got back."

"Back, back from where?" asked Henry with a blank look.

"Haven't you heard?" asked Joe cautiously looking over his shoulder before turning back to him.

"Heard? Heard about what?" asked Henry, confused.

"About Beth Miller."

Henry shook his head perplexed.

"Beth Miller was murdered two nights ago by the Northeast Butcher. It's been on the news all day; I'm surprised you didn't hear about it?"

"I've been locked in my office since this morning working on the proposals for the new waterfront development, then came straight here," explained Henry.

"Busy day?"

"That's an understatement," declared Henry with a sigh then glanced at Joe. "So, where did it happen?"

"She was working part time at a boutique in a strip mall in Melrose Park, and went missing after her shift ended Saturday night, around nine. A couple of hikers found her body early the following morning in a small clearing in a dense wooded area next to a cemetery, just north of Auburn. She was living with her parents up in in Owasco."

"Melrose Park!" exclaimed Henry. "That's less than twenty miles northwest of here!"

"I know," said Joe calmly, "that's why it's under my jurisdiction."

"How old was she?"

"Eighteen," he replied, "just a teenager with her whole life ahead of her."

"Eighteen," repeated Henry shaking his head in disbelief. "How close are they to catching him?"

Joe leaned over and said quietly, "not close at all, there are no leads."

"No leads," Henry whispered back.

"This guy really knows what he's doing," stated Joe. "The heavy rain washed everything away, so there's no evidence of him even being there, except for the victim's body covered in mud and wet leaves. It's a million-to-one she was found!" Joc hesitated momentarily. "He is the serial killer of all serial killers!"

"What makes you say that?"

"Henry, this goes no further than you and me," said Joe warily looking around.

"I understand," replied Henry giving him a trustworthy look.

Joe slowly began. "He started back in January, in Rhode Island, killing a thirty-one-year-old female. In February, he went west to Connecticut, killing a thirty-four-year-old male. Then in March, he headed southwest through New York to New Jersey, murdering a woman twenty-nine, and seven days later, a girl twenty-one. In April, he continued on to Delaware, murdering a twenty-year-old male, and a week later in Maryland, a thirty-three-year-old female. Then in May, he went north to Pennsylvania, killing a twenty-three-year-old woman, and the following week, a twenty-seven-year-old man, before heading northeast to New York. Specifically, Melrose Park, to abduct and kill Beth Miller. She's the first in our state, and I'm afraid to say, probably not the last. They're saying he's going to head east, but if he decides to take the scenic route south around Skaneateles Lake rather than the I90, our town will be right in his path. After New York, the FBI is predicting he will go into Vermont, skip over into Maine, and then down into New Hampshire, before heading south to Massachusetts, to complete his circle."

"Do they think he's from Massachusetts?"

"Again, just between us, they believe he is, and that he's saving his home state for last. They've told the public they are trying to anticipate his path and are assuming that he will eventually end up back where he started, and hopefully they can catch him along the way, but nothing else."

"You mentioned something about a circle. Why a circle?"

"Who knows for sure with this guy," replied Joe tentatively, "but one thing is certain, it's not a coincidence."

"How do they even know it's the same person?" queried Henry.

"Because of the way the victims are murdered. He always uses the same killing ritual and leaves their bodies in very remote areas, and by the time they're found, most of them have been partially eaten by wild animals or decomposed beyond recognition. With the exception of the bodies, there's never a trace that he was even there. He's a sick bastard; but clever. In fact, I couldn't even tell you if the Northeast Butcher is a, he."

"Are you telling me Joe, he's killed a total of nine people, in seven states over the last six months, and they have nothing? Not even with Beth Miller?"

"Nothing, not a thing…which is why he is the serial killer of all serial killers," reiterated Joe, shaking his head, and looking despondently at the dead leaves rustling by him on the ground.

There was a long silence as they both thought about the Northeast Butcher.

Joe glanced up and spoke softly, "Henry, in most likelihood he's probably a hundred miles from Charlotte. But in all of the cases, the victims have been taken in the evening, when they're on their own, and most vulnerable. Just make sure you keep your girls close by."

"I will, they'll be safe with me," he said placing his hand appreciatively on Joe's shoulder and thanking him.

Joe smiled, he had two daughters of his own, and it was nice to have a best friend like Henry to confide in.

Henry removed his hand, looked over at the parents in the distance heading back inside, and changed the subject. "Are you enjoying the show?"

"Yeah, they're doing a fantastic job."

"They sure are."

They continued to talk about the play as they went inside. After Joe said goodbye, Henry sat back down next to Megan and Sam. The lights dimmed, and Stephanie and the cast came on to the stage to start the second act. As Henry looked on, the Darkness inside thought about how everything was quietly falling into place, and proudly smiled.

About the Author

Edgar Waldgrave lives in

the small, quaint town of Skaneateles,

Onondaga County, New York.

You can contact him on his website:

www.edgarwaldgrave.com

Or on Facebook:

Edgar Waldgrave

www.ingramcontent.com/pod-product-compliance
Lightning Source LLC
Chambersburg PA
CBHW021206110726
47900CB00002B/762